I0637234

I Have A Secret

TAMMY COCKRUM

I Have A Secret
Copyright © 2024 by Tammy Cockrum.

All rights reserved. No part of this publication may be reproduced, distributed, or transmitted in any form or by any means, including photocopying, recording, or other electronic or mechanical methods, without the written consent of the publisher. The only exceptions are for brief quotations included in critical reviews and other noncommercial uses permitted by copyright law.

MILTON & HUGO L.L.C.
4407-11 Park Ave., Suite 5
Union City, NJ 07087, USA

Website: *www. miltonandhugo.com*
Hotline: *1- 888-778-0033*
Email: *info@miltonandhugo.com*

Ordering Information:
Quantity sales. Special discounts are granted to corporations, associations, and other organizations. For more information on these discounts, please reach out to the publisher using the contact information provided above.

Library of Congress Control Number: IN-PROCESS
ISBN-13: 979-8-89285-017-9 [Paperback Edition]
979-8-89285-018-6 [Digital Edition]

Rev. date: 01/09/2024

Hey you, come here! Yes, you, come closer. I have a secret to tell. Did you know that lightning bugs are fairies in disguise? If you could see all that my eyes have seen ... Wondrous things! You wouldn't believe all I have to tell. Things like, did you know there are hundreds of different kinds of fae folk? That's what they called fairies in the old days. Here is how I learned these things.

I love to walk in the woods exploring. I could stay out in the woods for days. One day, I was resting up against a great big oak tree. I heard a little voice say, "Hello there, how are you?"

I arose and looked around to see where the voice was coming from. All of a sudden, a little creature walked right out of the tree! Her skin looked like tree bark. She had long braided green hair and big dark green eyes. She was absolutely one of the most beautiful creatures I have ever seen. I couldn't believe what I saw, and my mouth fell open in awe.

I stuttered, "He-he-hello."

She looked at me and said, "My name is Willow, and I'm a tree fairy."

I said, "Hello, my name is Tammy, and I'm human."

She giggled and said, "Oh, silly, I know what you are. We very rarely show ourselves to your kind. I have observed you for a long while now. I have seen you out here quite often. I can tell you love to be out in the woods. I believe you have a good spirit, and I can trust you to keep my secret."

"Yes. Oh yes, I won't tell."

Willow then said, "I have an essential task I must do. I need a human's help. Would you be interested?"

"Me? I would love to. May I ask, what is this task, and where will it lead us to?"

Willow said, "The task is to plant an extraordinary seed way down deep in the middle of the earth. We fairies must do this every half a century. No flowers or fruit would bloom if we didn't, harming the earth and its creatures."

"Oh no, that would not be good at all. Of course, I want to help."

5

Willow then said, "Well, we leave today. We first travel by air, then by sea, and over the mountains. Then we travel deep into the ground to the middle of the earth."

"Wait, what? How will we go by sea? And did you say air? Oh no, to what have I agreed?"

"Oh, come, come, all will be well, you will see."

"What? Don't we even need to prepare?"

"Yes, now, and no preparation."

Willow then started climbing up that great big oak tree. I started climbing up behind her, and we didn't stop until we reached the tip-top.

Willow then began to sing in a language I have never heard: "Lolala lolalie lolalee."

"You have a lovely voice. What language were you singing in?"

"The very first language of the fae."

I then heard the fluttering sound of wings. I saw a little creature, kind of like Willow. With her big toe outstretched, she gracefully landed on the limb next to Willow. This creature was beautiful. She had pearl-white skin you could almost see through, long silver hair, great big sky-blue eyes, and wings.

Willow looked at me and said, "Emma is a sky fairy. She is going with us. We will need her help."

Emma said, "Hello, Tammy. It's nice to meet you."

"It is so very nice to meet you too."

Emma then started whistling the strangest-sounding whistle I had ever heard. Then there was a sound like thunder above us, and the sky grew dark. There were such strong gusts of wind that I almost fell out of the tree.

I hollered, "There's a storm coming. We had better take cover!"

I looked over at Willow and Emma. They were laughing at me and looking up. I looked up too and thought I could see a dragon ...

But no, dragons aren't real.

I looked again, and yes, it was a great big dragon! It was pearl white, and you could almost see through its skin like Emma's skin, but it had scales. This dragon was amazing to see.

Emma then hollered, "Hey, Mike, we need a ride to the sea."

Mike grumbled "Well, what are you waiting for? Let's go."

Emma asked him to throw down the ropes, which he did.

We all climbed up. When we reached the dragon, Emma said, "Mike, this is Tammy, and she is going with us."

Mike then said in a deep, rumbling voice, "Hello, Tammy, nice to meet you."

"It's very nice to meet you as well."

Mike then said, "Well, everybody, grab a seat and buckle up."

10

There were three saddles down along Mike's back and buckles that we could buckle around us, so we all took a seat.

Mike rumbled, "Hold on tight."

We took flight, going straight up. So high it looked as though we were in outer space. I felt as though I could reach out and touch a star. I saw the planets and the moon, and then we went straight down into a nosedive; and just when I thought we would crash into the water, we slowed down and glided into the sea.

Willow and Emma then began to make the strangest clicking noises with their mouths. When they finished, there emerged from the sea a little creature like them, but different.

She had shimmering skin of all different colors and hair the color of aqua blue and blue-green eyes that were quite mesmerizing. She had a tail like a dolphin's. She was quite something to see.

I was staring in awe when Willow and Emma introduced me and said Brenwehn was a sea fairy.

Brenwehn said, "Hello, Tammy, it's nice to meet you."

I said, "You as well."

Brenwehn then went under the water, and the water started moving in waves. It felt as though there were vibrations coming from the water, and then giant air bubbles started coming up as if the sea was boiling, which kind of scared me.

Then all of a sudden, this huge shiny silver snake-looking creature emerged. It had at least twenty-five big eyes down each side of its long body. They were purple, black, blue-green, and brown. They were beautiful—so different and strange.

Brenwehn then said, "Hello, Kye, my friends need a ride across the sea to the mountains. Would you take them for me?"

The creature blinked at her and bobbed his head.

Brenwehn then said, "Willow and Emma already know Kye." She then spoke to the creature. "Kye, this is Tammy."

I said, "Hello, Kye."

He blinked and bobbed his head. Mike then rumbled, "Hello, Kye," and Kye blinked and bobbed his head. Then he opened his mouth, and Willow and Emma climbed in.

They turned to me and said, "Come on, Tammy."

I looked at Brenwehn and said, "I don't know about that. I'm scared."

She said, "Oh no, don't be. Kye doesn't speak, but he is very sweet."

I said, "Okay, I will give it a try."

Brenwehn said, "You will be glad you did for all the wonderful things you are about to see."

I climbed in, and we took a seat as though we were on a train. Each of the eyes I had seen were like windows, and we could see everything around us. We then began to move through the sea smoothly and swiftly. I was in awe of all the beautiful things I saw. There were whales with their babies swimming right alongside them. Dolphins and sharks, even an octopus jellyfish too. I saw cities like the ones we have on land. It was the homes of the sea fairies like Brenwehn. They swam in and out and all around their beautiful city. It was wonderful to see.

Then we shifted, and I could see we started going up and up and up. We must have been at the bottom of the sea. It felt as though we had traveled straight up for at least an hour. I felt us pop up, and then soon we were floating on top of the sea. We then slithered onto the land, and Kye opened his mouth and we all got out onto land. I saw Brenwehn swimming about. Then she stood up and walked on land. Her tail was gone, and in its place, she had legs.

I said, "Hey, how did you do that?"

She laughed and said, "We fae folk have magic, didn't you know?"

"I did not, but I do now."

I looked up and around. Before my eyes were mountains that looked as though they touched the sky. I looked at the others and said, "It will take us a week to climb those mountains. Why can't we just fly?"

Willow said, "Oh no, we can't do that. There is a magic spell that stops anything from flying over the mountains. It has to be part of our task. We must be strong enough to climb the mountains to prove we are worthy enough for the task."

Emma said, "We also must watch out for the brownies and sprites. They are tricky little things that will try and make us fall."

"What? Why?"

"They are tricksters, that's what they do. Come, come, we must be there by four more moons."

Willow and Emma began to climb, and Brenwehn said, "Now you, Tammy, I will climb behind you so you will be in the middle. That way, we can watch out for you. Climb exactly behind them, do what they do."

"Okay, but I have to admit, I'm a little scared."

"I know. You must be strong. All will be well."

We began to climb. It seemed as though we had been climbing forever.

I said, "I'm so thirsty and tired. Can we stop to rest for a while?"

Willow said, "We still have a ways to go before we can rest." She handed me a little bottle of green juice and said, "Just take a little sip."

"I'm really thirsty, though," I said.

She looked at me and said, "Just a sip. Really, I mean, just a sip."

"Okay." So I just took a sip and handed the bottle back.

All of a sudden, I felt as though I had drunk one hundred Red Bulls. I said, "Wow, okay, let's go climb faster. Let's go, let's go, go, go!"

Emma looked at me and then at Willow. Then she said, "You really shouldn't have given her that!"

"What? It was just a sip."

"Yes, but, Willow, she's human, so it will affect her much stronger than it does us. When it wears off, she is going to be so tired."

Willow said, "Oh no, it will be fine. Come on, let's go."

I heard Willow holler, "Ooh!"

Then Emma hollered, "Ah!"

I asked, "What's the matter?"

And right then, out of nowhere, a little sparkly fairy jumped out where my right hand was and said, "Boo!" Then an ugly little brown creature jumped out where my left hand was and said, "Boo! Boo!"

I almost fell. "What in the world are those!"

Willow and Emma hollered, "Sprites and brownies."

"Oh, so that's what they do. That's kind of mean. Why do they do that?"

"It's part of our task. We must go through a test of our strength."

"Oh, I see. Why is the sprite so cute and sparkly while the brownies are so brown and ugly?"

Willow said, "Well, brownies are actually sprites that have lost their glitter."

Emma said, "Their happiness."

"Oh, you mean they are really depressed sprites?"

"Yes, actually, that is exactly what they are."

Then I heard Brenwehn below me growl, and I knew they were jumping out at her too. We climbed for a long while more. Then Emma said, "We will stop at that cave above us for the night. We will eat, rest, then we will finish the rest of our climb tomorrow."

We all agreed. "Sounds good."

I barely got a little food and watered down before I was snoring.

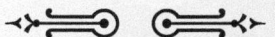

Emma said, "She is out like a light."

Brenwehn then said, "My goodness, how will we sleep with all that noise!"

They all laughed and bedded down for the night.

The next morning, I was awakened by the clanging sounds of pots and pans.

Willow said, "Wake up, sleepyhead. We have been trying to wake you for an hour at least."

"Oh goodness, I'm so sorry. I guess I was really tired."

"Well, get up and let's have breakfast. Then we must be off on our way."

We all ate and then started the rest of our climb first thing. The sprites and brownies were jumping out hollering, "Boo!"

You could hear us all growling as we climbed and laughing at one another. We climbed for the rest of the day, stopping a few times to catch our breath. That evening, we made it to the top of the mountains. You could reach out and touch the clouds. The mountains really did reach the sky. We ate and drank, told stories, and laughed. We then bedded down for the night.

The next morning, we all jumped up. We had been awakened by the sounds of pots and pans clanging together, thanks to the sprites and brownies. We all started mumbling and growling, and then laughed at one another. Our hair was standing straight up on top of our heads, thanks to the sprites and brownies. They had put pine goop in our hair. We giggled at one another for a while.

Then Willow said, "Come on, I know where there is a stream. We can wash up and wash this stuff out of our hair. It's on the way to where we are going. We didn't even eat breakfast because we couldn't quit laughing at one another. We started walking, still laughing, all the way. We saw the stream, and we all jumped in. We then started scrubbing the pine goop out of our hair. Then we just sat with our feet in the stream for a while. It felt so good on our tired, worn-out feet.

Emma then jumped up and said, "Goodness me, it's time to go. We have no more time to waste."

Willow said, "Oh yes, we must go. Go, hurry, or we will be late."

Brenwehn said, "Oh no, we can't be late!"

So we took off in a hurry down a dirt path. We followed the dirt path for quite a while. Then we came upon some caves.

Brenwehn said, "That's it, the one in the middle."

We walked to the middle cave and walked into it. Then we walked deeper into the cave. We couldn't see light from the outside anymore, so it was really dark and scary.

I said, "Oh no, guys, I'm not going any farther."

Then we saw the light deeper in the cave.

Willow said, "Come on, that's how we need to go."

So we walked toward the light. As we got close, it looked like a fire. Then we walked closer, and the fire started moving our way. I looked at the others. They were not bothered by this, so I said, "Okay."

Then before me stood this magnificent creature. I couldn't believe my eyes. This creature was made of fire and stood six feet tall. Her skin was the lightest blue flame, and her hair was long red flames that hung to the ground. She was beautiful and terrifying at the same time.

When she spoke, it sounded as though she had a megaphone held to her mouth. It was loud and vibrated all throughout the cave.

She said, "I am a fire fairy. My name is Shoshana, and I am the guardian of all paths that lead to the middle of the earth. Who are the ones who stand before me now, and what is your reason for taking this path?"

29

Willow spoke up. "We are the ones that have taken on the task that must be done every half century."

Shoshana then said, "So you carry the very special seed pod. I know of this task. Would each of you step forward and tell me your name, species, and your part of the task."

Willow said, "Yes, of course. I am Willow, a tree fairy that must plant the pod in the earth."

Then Brenwehn stepped forward and said, "I am Brenwehn, a sea fairy that must water the pod."

Emma stepped forward and said, "I am Emma, a sky fairy that will call down the light that must shine on the pod."

Then they all turned and looked at me. I stepped up and said, "I am Tammy, a human, but I do not yet know my task."

Shoshana looked at Willow and said, "You have not told her what she must do?"

Willow said, "No, not yet. I thought it would be easier to explain when we got here."

Shoshana said, "Well, what are you waiting for?"

Willow then turned to me and said, "The pod will need your breath. You will just blow on it."

I looked at her and said, "That's all? That's easy enough."

Shoshana said, "I am honored to meet you all and happy to see you all here for this wonderful very important task. Now you all still have a little ways to go to reach the middle of the earth. I will introduce you to your guides, who will show you the way. You all will need their guidance. The path is forever changing and can be very tricky. These guys are forever watching. It's what they do—they monitor everything that goes on down here and know the exact time and place that the pod needs to be planted."

Shoshana then said, "Boys, come meet the ladies that you will be guiding for every half century's middle of the earth's very special seed pod planting."

Then up walked two of the shortest, cutest little fellows I have ever seen. Shoshana introduced them. "This is Cody, and this is Jacob. They are dwarfs and brothers. They are the caretakers of the middle of the earth."

They bowed and said, "Hello, ladies, it's so nice to meet you."

Cody then stepped up and said, "If you ladies are ready, we have no time to waste."

Willow said, "Yes, we are ready."

Jacob said, "Let us be on our way. Come follow us. This is the way."

We followed the little cuties. I mean, they were just so cute I couldn't get over it. We had been walking for a little while when the boys started arguing back and forth and stopped a few paces ahead of us.

Cody would say, "It's this way."

Then Jacob said, "No, it's this way."

Cody said, "No, you're wrong. You are being a stubborn goat."

Jacob said, "No, you're wrong, and I'll teach you to call me a goat."

Then they started rolling around on the ground and kicking at each other. Then all of a sudden, they both jumped up and said, "We missed that path. We were both wrong. That's the way."

Then they started singing a silly little tune:

Oh yes, we're the best

Better than all the rest

They can put us to the test

And we never have to guess

Because we're the best

Then they bumped chest and dusted themselves off and said, "Come, ladies. This way."

We walked a while more. Then we entered an oval-looking cave, which had a big dip in the middle of the floor.

The boys pointed and said, "This is where it's supposed to be planted."

I got so excited I couldn't believe we finally made it to where we were to plant the seed pod. I was so happy I couldn't stand still.

"Well, let's do it. What are we waiting for?"

Willow looked at me. "Tammy, you must calm down. This is a ritual, and it must be peaceful and purposeful."

"Okay, I'm sorry. I will be calm."

Willow then walked to the middle of the oval cave where there was a dip in the ground. She then took the leather pouch from her side and pulled out the seed pod. She placed it in the dip in the ground and then said, "I am Willow, a tree fairy, and I plant the seed and give it my growth power." She then covered the seed with soil.

Then Brenwehn stepped up and said, "I am a sea fairy, and I give it the water of life." And water came forth from her hand.

Then Emma stepped up and said, "I am Emma, a sky fairy, and I call on the queen of the lightning bug fairies. Queen Tylor, will you please come with all your lightning bug fairies and grant us your light so that the seed pod will bloom."

We all sat and waited for about twenty minutes. Then we heard the loudest swarm of little wings you could ever imagine. There were millions of what I thought were lightning bugs. They all landed, and then one moved toward us and started removing her legs and head. I then saw all that was armor, and there was actually a very tiny fairy underneath all of that armor, and the part where lightning bugs glow is just a little clear sack where they put their pixie dust. See, I told you lightning bugs were fairies in disguise.

The little queen then bowed and said, "I am Tylor, the queen of lightning bug fairies, and we are here to give our magical light." Tylor then turned to the lightning bugs and said, "Okay, my royal army, let's shake those tails and make that pixie dust glow."

And they did, and it was almost blinding. It was beautiful, so sparkly and bright. Then a little sprout popped out of the ground, and we all gasped. Then everyone looked at me and said, "Tammy, it is now your turn."

I walked over to the small sprout and said, "I am Tammy, a human, and I give my breath."

I bent down and blew on the sprout, and it started growing into a huge bud and then bloomed right before our eyes. It was so beautiful and amazing. It was a flower with petals of every color you could imagine, and each petal was a different shape. It was the most wonderful and unique thing I have ever seen.

So now when you see a flower bloom or a fruit on a tree, you know the secret behind it. But be sure not to tell.

THE END

www.ingramcontent.com/pod-product-compliance
Lightning Source LLC
Chambersburg PA
CBHW041539240626
47164CB00002B/66